PIG the PUG

This book belongs to:

PIG the PUG

For my parents.
And all those little dogs.

ISBN 978-1-338-16647-7

10 9 8 7 6 5 4 3 2   17 18 19 20 21

Printed in the U.S.A.   08
First printing 2017

The artwork in this book is acrylic (with pens and pencils) on watercolor paper.
The type was set in Adobe Caslon.

PIG the PUG

Aaron Blabey

Scholastic Inc.

Pig was a pug
and I'm sorry to say,
he was greedy and selfish
in most every way.

He lived in a house
with a wiener dog, Trevor.
But when was he nice to him?
I'll tell you—**NEVER**.

"You've got some great toys there,"
poor Trevor would say.

But Pig would just grumble,
"They're mine! **GO AWAY!**"

"But it might be more fun," Trevor said to Pig,
"if we both played together . . ."

Well, Pig flipped his wig.

"No, they are mine!
Didn't you hear? Only mine!
You keep your paws off them,
they are mine, mine, mine!

I know what your game is,
you want me to **SHARE!**
But I'll never do that!
I WON'T and **I SWEAR!**"

And with that, he proceeded to gather his stuff

and make a big pile, with a huff and a puff.

And once he had gathered them
up in a pile,
he howled from the top
with a satisfied smile.

"There!" shouted Pig.
"Now you won't get my loot!
It's **MINE! MINE! MINE! MINE!**
So why don't you **SCOOT**?"

But just at that moment,
poor Trevor did see
the pile was wobbling.

Oh dear me.

"Watch out up there!" good Trevor did cry.
But the shame of it was . . .

Well, pugs cannot fly.

These days it's different,
I'm happy to say.
It's so very different
in most every way.

Yes, Pig shares his toys now,
and Trevor's his friend.
And they both play together . . .

. . . while Pig's on the mend.